**CLEVER**
• Publishing •

Text copyright © 2021 by **Elena Feldman**
Illustrations copyright © 2021 by **Mary Koless**

First published in the United States of America in August 2022 by "Clever-Media-Group" LLC
www.clever-publishing.com

ISBN 978-1-954738-46-1 (hardcover)

For information about permission to reproduce selections from this book, write to:
CLEVER PUBLISHING
79 MADISON AVENUE; 8TH FLOOR
NEW YORK, NY 10016

For general inquiries, contact: info@clever-publishing.com
CLEVER is a registered trademark of "Clever-Media-Group" LLC

To place an order for Clever Publishing books, please contact The Quarto Group:
sales@quarto.com • Tel: (+1) 800-328-0590

Art created with Procreate and Adobe Photoshop
Book design by Michelle Martinez
MANUFACTURED, PRINTED, AND ASSEMBLED IN CHINA

10 9 8 7 6 5 4 3 2 1

CHRISTMAS
in the
FOREST

by Elena Feldman

illustrated by Mary Koless

 CLEVER Publishing

The animals of Evergreen Forest LOVE Christmas!
It's their favorite time of year, because they get
to play in the SNOW!

Everyone goes sledding, has snowball fights,
and makes snow angels.

But this year, there's no snow! So the animals gathered near the largest Christmas tree in the forest to talk about what to do.

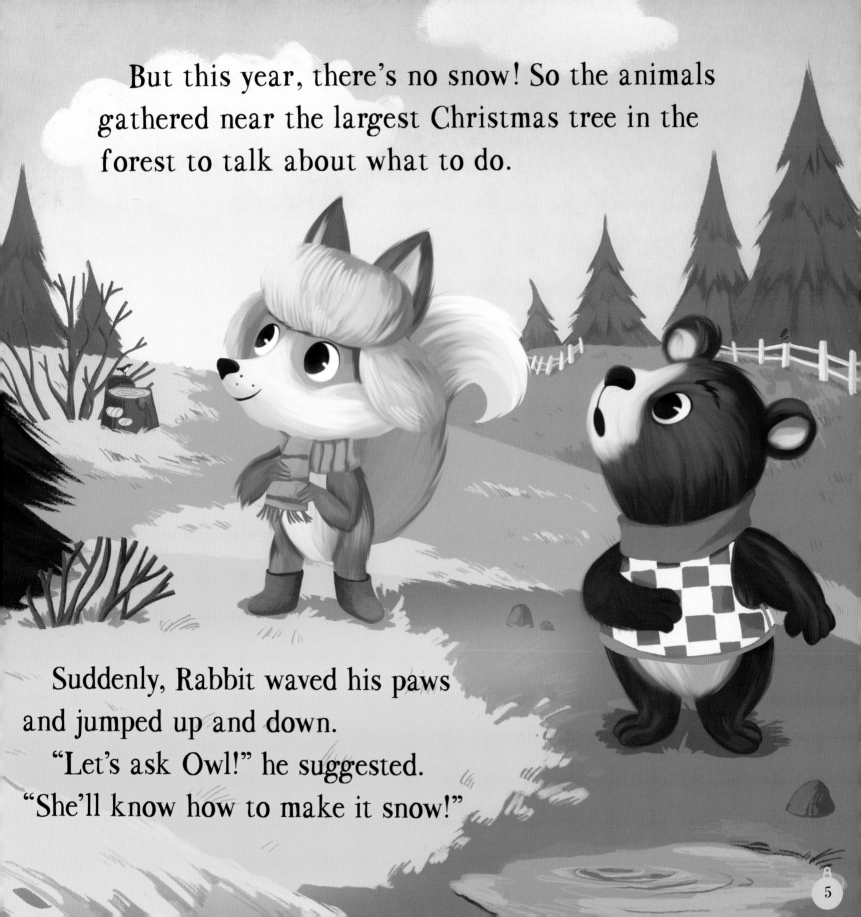

Suddenly, Rabbit waved his paws and jumped up and down.

"Let's ask Owl!" he suggested. "She'll know how to make it snow!"

The animals knocked on Owl's door.

KNOCK! KNOCK!

There was no answer.

WELCOME TO OWL'S HOUSE.
you see this sign,
I'm sleeping. Please do not
sturb, but me back later!

So they knocked louder: KNOCK! KNOCK!

Again, there was no answer

Can you knock even louder?

KNOCK! KNOCK! KNOCK!

WELCOME TO OWL'S HOUSE.
If you see this sign, I'm sleeping. Please do not disturb—but come back later!

The door finally opened, and Owl slowly peered outside.

"What is all the noise?" she asked sleepily. "I was trying to sleep!"

"We're sorry," Bear said, "but we need your help! Do you know how to make it snow?"

"We need to blow into the air," Owl suggested.

"Why?" asked Bear.

"How do you cool down hot soup?" Owl replied.

"Oh!" Bear smiled. "I blow on it!"

"That's right," Owl said. "So if we blow into the air, we just might make it cold enough to snow!"

The animals gathered in a circle and began to blow.

Can you blow with the animals?
WHOOOOO!
WHOOOOO!

But that didn't work.
It didn't start to snow.

"Let's try singing a song about snow," said Owl.

Sing with the animals!

LET IT SNOW!
LET IT SNOW!

LET THE WINDS
THROUGH THE
FOREST BLOW!

SNOWSTORMS AND
DRIFTS ARE NEAR,

SANTA CLAUS IS
ALMOST HERE!

It was a very good song,
and everyone sang their best.
But there still was no snow!

"Hmm," said Owl. "I think we need to do the dance of the snowflakes! The snowflakes will look at us from above and decide to join us in our winter celebration."

The animals were delighted and started dancing, swinging their paws and spinning all around.

Can you dance with the animals?

SWING YOUR ARMS AND SPIN AROUND!

It was a wonderful dance! Owl even played her violin.
But not a single snowflake fell from the sky.

Owl sighed. "I thought for sure that would work!" she said. "I have one last idea. Squirrel, climb to the top of the tallest tree and tickle the cloud's belly. That will make her laugh, and snow will fall from the sky!"

Help Squirrel tickle the cloud!

HEE HEE HEE!

HAA HAA HAA!

TICKLE!
TICKLE!

So Squirrel tickled the cloud until she laughed,
but there STILL was no snow anywhere!

"We've tried everything, but nothing has worked," Bear said.
"Now we won't be able to make snowmen, have snowball fights,
or make snow angels," sighed Squirrel.
"Without snow, it just won't feel like Christmas,"
Rabbit added sadly.

Suddenly, Fox remembered something and ran to his house.

"My mom has something that might help us!"

he shouted.

SHUFFLE! SHUFFLE!

"Yay!" the other animals cheered.

"Go get it!"

Fox came back with a magic snow globe that had a snowman in it. He gently shook the globe up and down.

Shake the snow globe with Fox!

SHAKE! SHAKE!

Wow! It's starting to snow!

Shake the snow globe harder!

"Uh-oh!" cried Squirrel.
"Now there's TOO much snow!"

Tip the book from side to side
to shake off the extra snow.

UP, DOWN . . .

LEFT, RIGHT!

PERFECT!

The animals were so happy
to have snow.

Squirrel and Rabbit built a
snowman. Bear and Fox had a snowball
fight. And Owl began decorating the Christmas tree.

Soon, it was dark in the forest. The animals gathered around the tree in their sleeping bags to wait for Santa Claus to come.

"Thank you, Owl, for such good ideas," Rabbit whispered.
Owl looked puzzled. "But they didn't help at all," she replied.
"Yes, they did!" said Bear. "You put us in a Christmas mood,
and we had fun together. That's more important to us than
having snow."

Later that night, when all of the animals were asleep, Santa Claus came! He left presents for everyone near the tree. Then he tiptoed back to his sleigh and flew off into the chilly winter night.

In the morning, the animals woke up to a pile of presents.
"Oh, wow!" exclaimed Rabbit. "Santa came!"
"THIS IS THE BEST CHRISTMAS EVER!"
they all cheered.